amoeba

aardvark

cat

bat

polar bear

hedgehog

shark

slug

pig

puffin

moose

dolphin

dog

snail

pig

duck billed platypus

spider

armadillo

To Ivy
with love, Berny
BS

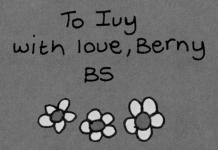

Text and Illustration copyright © 1996 bang on the door™
Style and design of all titles in the bang on the door™ series
copyright © 1996 bang on the door™
bang on the door™ is a registered trademark.

Karen Duncan, Samantha Stringle, Jackie Robb, and Berny Stringle
assert their moral right to be identified as the authors of this work.

First published in the United States in 1997 by Price Stern Sloan, Inc.
A member of The Putnam & Grosset Group,
New York, New York.

First published in the United Kingdom by David Bennett Books Ltd.

ISBN 0-8431-7930-9

First Edition
1 3 5 7 9 10 8 6 4 2

Library of Congress Catalog Number: 96-69523

Production by Imago
Printed in Singapore

bat

Created by bang on the door™

Illustrated by
Karen Duncan and Samantha Stringle

Story by
Jackie Robb and Berny Stringle

PRICE STERN SLOAN
Los Angeles

Bat never followed fashion
he wasn't very cool,

The fact that he was different was the cause of ridicule.

Bat was seen as batty
even by his closest friends,

Until his style of dressing
started setting fashion trends.

Take the craze for baggy pants
and the backwards baseball hat,

Accidental fashion firsts—
introduced by Bat.

these jeans
used to be huge

Bat spiked his hair and
dyed it green
and pulled on jeans he'd shrunk,

Then thrashed an out-of-tune guitar
and called the music punk.

Bat liked to jog and cycle
wearing skin-tight purple shorts,

Now every athlete in the land
is wearing them for sports.

Bat pioneered the "country look"— checked shirt and dungarees,

And caused a fashion frenzy
when he cut holes in the knees.

Smelly clothes

His next new style they labeled grunge
which frankly is a mess,

Bat's studded leather jacket became standard biker's dress.

Kids raved about his footwear
which always matched his suits,

They went wild about his sneakers
and his black construction boots.

Everybody copied Bat:
Mr. What-to-Wear,

He dreamed about the old days when they used to laugh and stare.

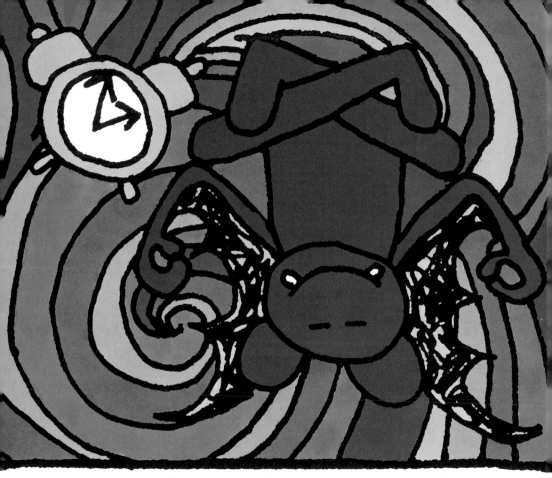

So Bat began to meditate
and chanted for two hours,

Then threw out his trendy clothes
and danced among the flowers.

Wearing nothing but his love beads
Bat flew down to Mississippi,

Where he hung out upside-down and the locals called him "Hippie."

But followers of fashion
came in from every town,

And guess what they are doing?
Hanging upside-down!